This Book Belongs To

· ·

Published by Tate Publishing & Enterprises, LLC
127 E. Trade Center Terrace | Mustang, Oklahoma 73064 USA
1.888.361.9473 | www.tatepublishing.com

Tate Publishing is committed to excellence in the publishing industry. The company reflects the philosophy established by the founders, based on Psalm 68:11,
"The Lord gave the word and great was the company of those who published it."

Book design copyright © 2011 by Tate Publishing, LLC. All rights reserved.
Cover and interior design by Chris Webb
Illustrations by Glori Alexander

Published in the United States of America

ISBN: 978-1-61777-584-0
1. Juvenile Fiction / Social Issues / Self-Esteem & Self-Reliance
2. Juvenile Fiction / Stories In Verse
11.09.27

Left Out Lucie

tate publishing
CHILDREN'S DIVISION

written by
MARYBETH HARRISON

Every day it happened
At recess around noon.
Lucie dreaded going out.
Lunchtime came too soon.

Teams were picked for kickball,
And everybody knew
Lucie would get picked last.
She felt so sad and blue.

All the kids ignored her.
Why couldn't they see?
Lucie didn't like kickball.
Why not just let her be?

She couldn't stay inside
Although Lucie wished she could.
The rules were to play outdoors,
So she did as she should!

As Lucie stood in the outfield,
She wished the time would fly.
No one *ever* kicked the ball to her.
It was so hard not to cry.

As she waited for the ball
Lucie turned to see
Some girls were jumping rope.
Lucie leapt with glee!

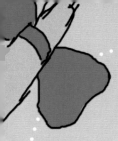

Lucie *loooved* jumping rope.
She practiced every day.
Just then, Lucie promised herself
No more kickball would she play.

The next day Lucie brought a game
to share with everyone.
All the girls looked at Lucie.
They were ready for some fun.

Sparkly purple and glittery pink,
Her jump ropes were so cool.
Lucie was so happy.
No more kickball at school!

Double Dutch and red hot pepper,
Lucie knew them all.
Some of the kids began to watch.
They even forgot about kickball!

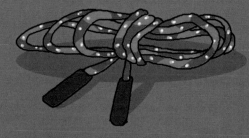

The kids on the field
Were amazed by Lucie's skill.
Everyone wanted to watch her.
For Lucie, it was a thrill!

So no more "left-out" Lucie.
Jumping rope helped her through.
Always keep trying new things
And discover what YOU like to do!

e|LIVE

listen|imagine|view|experience

AUDIO BOOK DOWNLOAD INCLUDED WITH THIS BOOK!

In your hands you hold a complete digital entertainment package. In addition to the paper version, you receive a free download of the audio version of this book. Simply use the code listed below when visiting our website. Once downloaded to your computer, you can listen to the book through your computer's speakers, burn it to an audio CD or save the file to your portable music device (such as Apple's popular iPod) and listen on the go!

How to get your free audio book digital download:

1. Visit www.tatepublishing.com and click on the e|LIVE logo on the home page.
2. Enter the following coupon code:
   ea56-7237-dd85-e9dc-48e6-967b-38c6-570e
3. Download the audio book from your e|LIVE digital locker and begin enjoying your new digital entertainment package today!